EWE

DISNEY · HYPERION

LOS ANGELES   NEW YORK

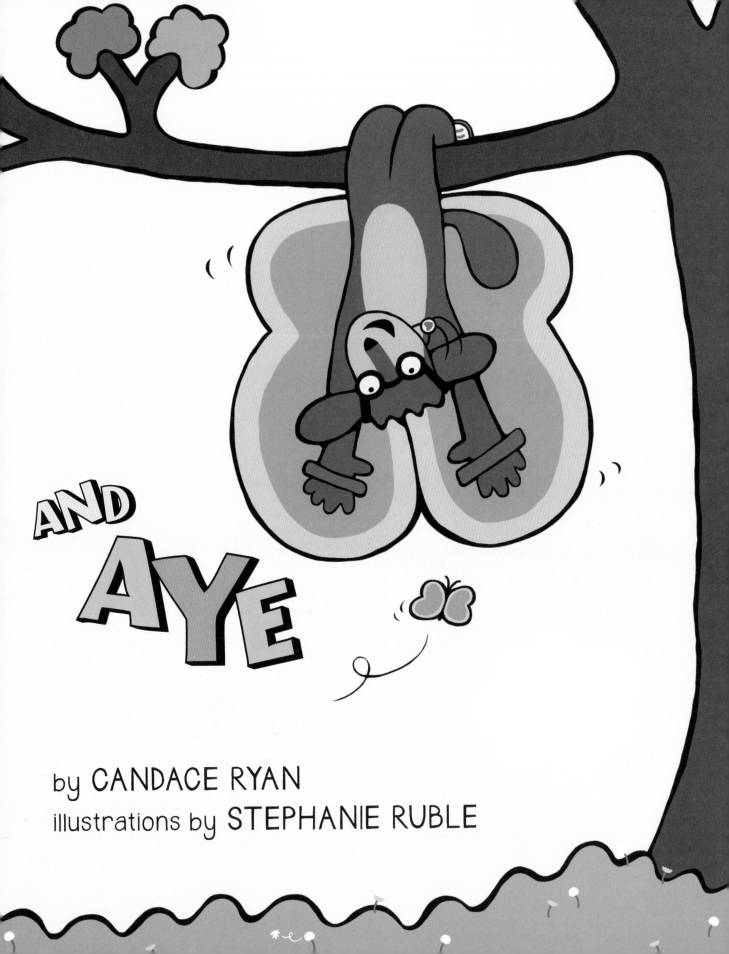

AND
AYE

by CANDACE RYAN
illustrations by STEPHANIE RUBLE

Ewe and Aye were different.

Ewe loved wheels,
and Aye loved wings.

But Ewe and Aye both
dreamed of flying.

"WEEEEEEE

One day,
Ewe got an idea,

and Aye had a plan.

and Aye got flat tired.

Then Ewe had a plan,

and Aye got an idea.

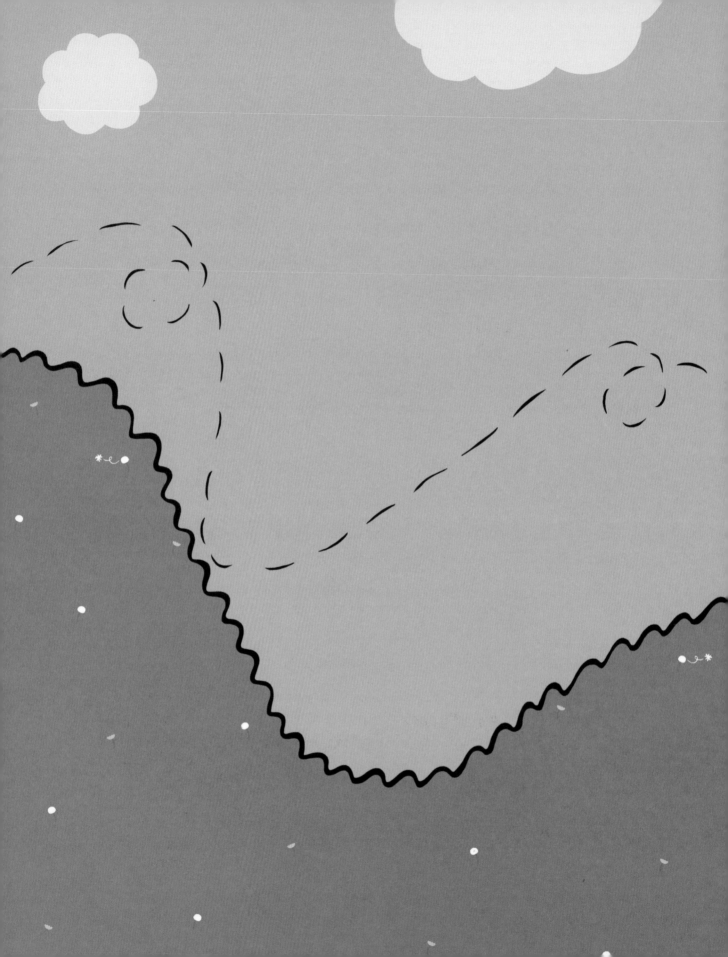

and Aye couldn't let go.

Then one day when Ewe got into trouble,
Aye was there to help.

And when Aye got stuck,
Ewe came to the rescue.

It wasn't long before Ewe and Aye
talked about flying—

how Ewe could never
get high enough,

"WEEE

and how Aye could never
hold tight enough.

"EEEEEE!"

So, Ewe and Aye got an idea

there's nowhere Ewe and Aye can't fly.

and made a new plan.

Ewe and Aye.

And now together . . .

WE!

For Doug Hannah, guileless guide and
guardian to all who dream of flying —C.R.

To M & D, who always encouraged my art
and imagination —S.R.

Text copyright © 2014 by Candace Ryan
Illustrations copyright © 2014 by Stephanie Ruble

Printed in Malaysia

First Edition
10 9 8 7 6 5 4 3 2 1
H106-9333-5-14227

Library of Congress Cataloging-in-Publication Data
Ryan, Candace. Ewe and Aye / by Candace Ryan ; illustrations by Stephanie Ruble.—First edition.
    pages cm
Summary: Ewe and Aye are very different but both dream of flying, so when Ewe's love of
wheels and Aye's knowledge of wings come together they finally get off the ground.
ISBN 978-1-4231-7591-9
[1. Flight—Fiction. 2. Cooperativeness—Fiction. 3. Individuality—Fiction. 4. Sheep—Fiction.
5. Lemurs—Fiction.] I. Ruble, Stephanie, illustrator. II. Title. III. Title: Ewe & Aye.
PZ7.R9477Ewe 2014 [E]—dc23 2013046183
Designed by Kevin Lewis
Reinforced binding

Visit www.DisneyBooks.com